This book belongs to

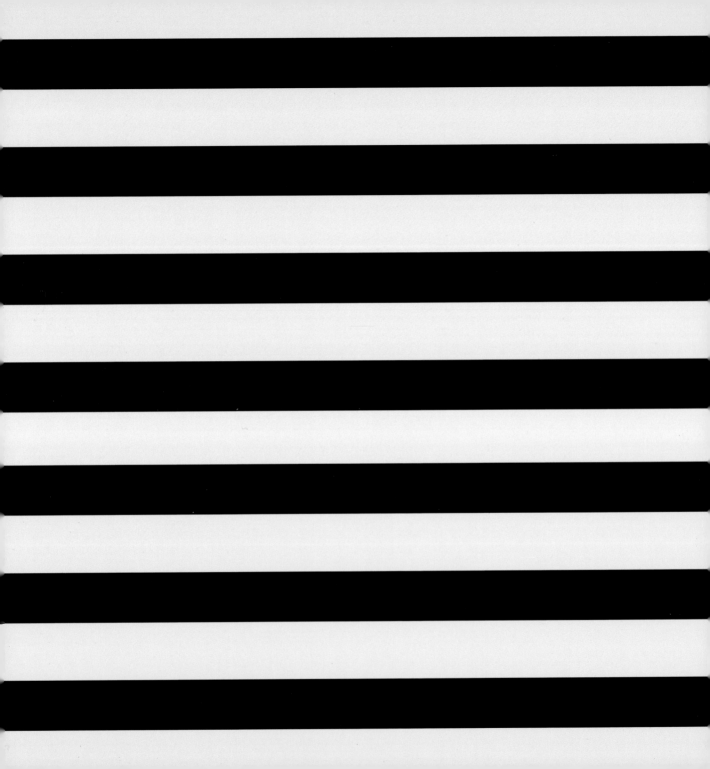

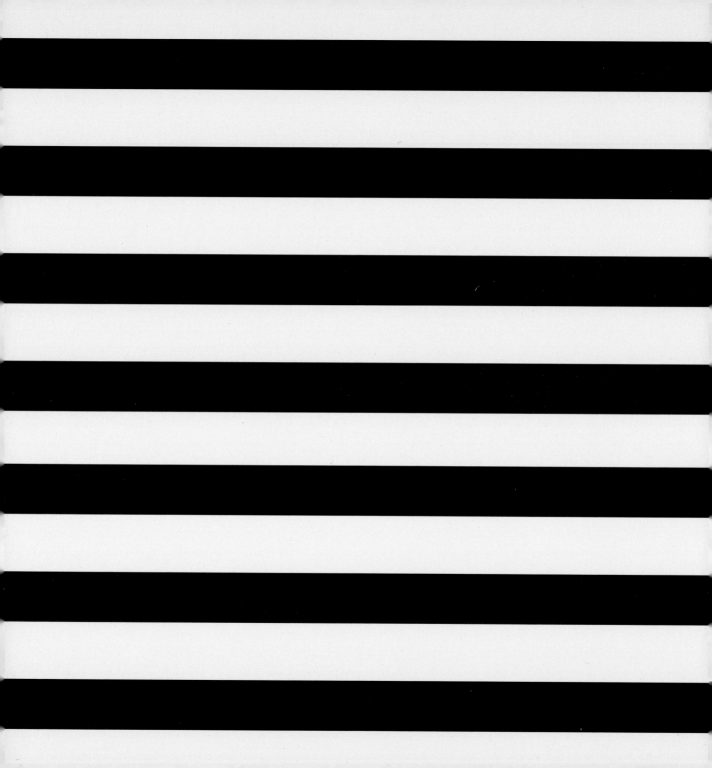

Written by Katherine Walker.
Illustrated by Beverley Hopwood.

Beekind

Beverley Hopwood · Katherine Walker

make
believe
ideas

Ben was having a bad day.
He was **really** down in the **dumps.**
He **didn't** want to Share his toys,
and SO he got the **grumps.**

He hadn't **felt** like being kind
when his **sister** asked to **play.**
So when **Mom** said, "It's Bella's turn!"
he **Sulked** and **ran away.**

He **stomped** out to the **garden** and **pulled** up all the plants! He **stamped** on all the **flowers**

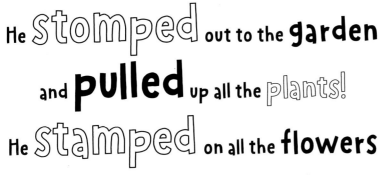

in a **furious,** **frenzied** **dance.**

Buzzing through the bushes
was Beelinda the honeybee.
She'd seen the fuss that morning
and had watched Ben carefully.

Beelinda flew to find her friends –
the buzzy honey crew.

"Let's show **Ben** that being **kind**

is **something** he **must** do."

They **sprinkled** magic pollen from their **fuzzy, buzzy knees** all over **Ben**, who **scrunched** his nose as he began to **sneeze!**

Every time **Ben** shrieked –

"Achoo!" –

he became a little less tall.

He **spluttered,**

wheezed,

and **sneezed** until

he was **really,**

really

small!

First Ben felt a little scared, then Beelinda said, "Grab my wings. Come with me, and I'll show you a bee's-eye view of things."

Beelinda and Ben skimmed over puddles
that looked like massive lakes.
They whizzed past towering toadstools
and worms the size of snakes!

On they flew through flowery forests,
as big birds filled the sky.
They swooped past sticky spiderwebs,
as huge hares hopped right by.

"Welcome!" said Beelinda, as they **buzzed** up to a tree. "This is where I **live** and **work**, with other honeybees!"

"You all **work together**," said **Ben**, "like one **big family.**"

Beelinda said,

"There's **one more** thing

I think you **need** to **see**."

"Trees and flowers need our help,
so when we're on the go,
we spread their pollen all around –
it helps more plants to grow!"

Then small **Ben remembered** how unkind he'd been **before.** **Bee**linda had taught him lots of things he couldn't just **ignore.**

"I need to **share** with **Bella**,

and **work together** to improve.

I'll **show her** all the things I've learned . . .
and how **bees** move and groove!"

HONEY

"When it comes to kindness, I can **see** you've got it **right**.
I'm going to **be** a bit more **bee** when I'm back to normal height!"

Bee**linda** saw that **Ben** had learned,

and he wanted to make a **change**.

So she gave him a taste of **honey**,

and he started to **feel** a bit strange . . .

His **body** began to tingle,
then his **limbs** started
to **grow.**

Soon he was **back** to **Ben size** –
stretched out from **head to toe!**

Now any time **Ben** plays with **Bella**,
his **bee friends** buzz to mind.

He **remembers** all he **learned** that day,
and he always tries to **bee kind.**

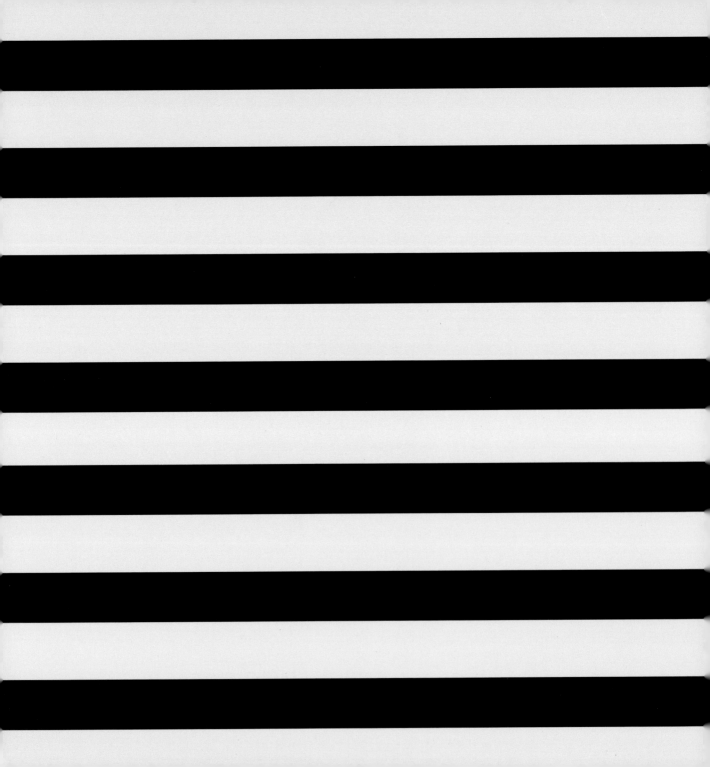

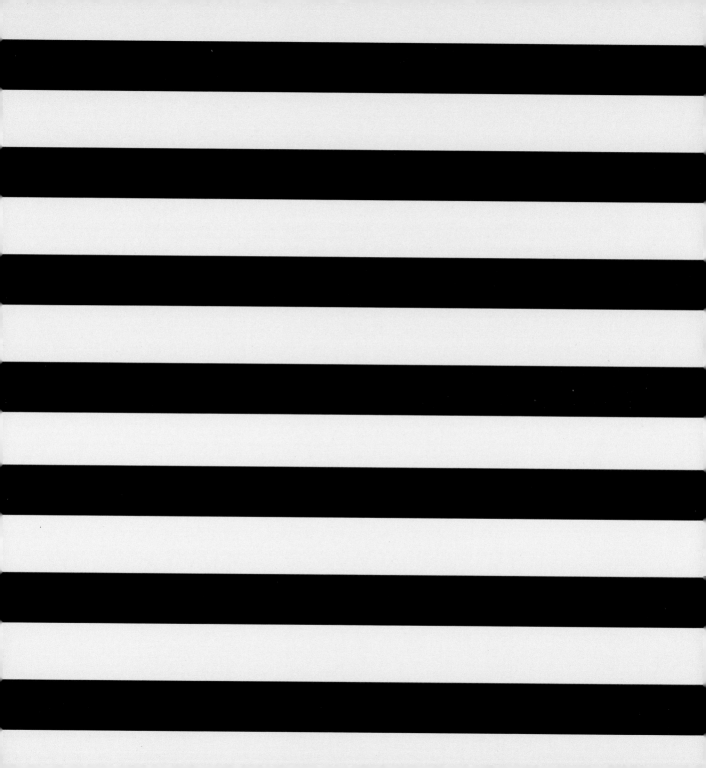

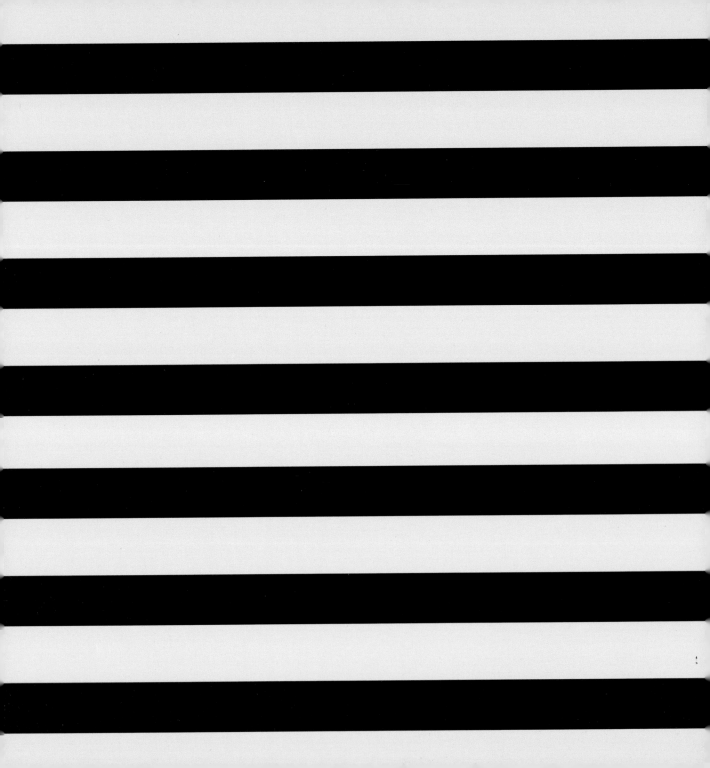